Gypsies in Training

Written and Illustrated by

Jacqueline Fowler

D1567636

Gypsies in Training

For my parents who inspired me to write, write, write
and for my sister who reads my books whenever she can

Prologue

You may remember the last time we met Nicole Ruby, a sweet eight year old girl with a wild imagination. She made a wish to Madam Lavender, a magical circus gypsy[1] to have long hair like her best friend Monique. That wish was granted but led to some terrible consequences.

To her great delight, the gypsy granted her wish. However, Nicole learned a valuable lesson about making wishes to gypsies: you have to be very careful to give the gypsy your exact request. Nicole asked Madam Lavender for "hair as long as Rapunzel." Just like Rapunzel, Nicole's hair would not stop growing! Within one school day, her hair was all the way down to her toes!

---

[1] *A member of a people that arrived in Europe in migrations from Northern India*

Since her adventure last year, Nicole has been reading all sorts of gypsy books like crazy. She learned how to mix magic potions, speak the gypsy language and dress like a gypsy. She is still working on figuring out what the secret ingredient is, and how to change the flavors of the potions.

Chapter 1: The Circus is Coming Back

One morning when Nicole was walking to the school bus stop, she found a strange looking paper on the ground. It was crumbled and dirty, but Nicole could barely make out what is said. The paper read:

Cirque du Mystere is coming back to your town!

Date: June 5-6, 2010

Location: Buttercup Meadow

"Oh my gosh. The circus is coming back!" Nicole said as she folded the paper carefully and put it in her pocket. "I better tell Monique."

"Oh my!" said Monique, "I have never been to the circus! I really wanted to go after you told me your secret story about Madam Lavender. Maybe I can meet the gypsy too!"

"I hope you can," said Nicole, beaming. "I am so anxious for school to be over."

"Me too!" exclaimed Monique.

"Why don't you stop over at my house after school? I have lots of helpful gypsy books."

"These books are amazing!" said Monique, who was reading a book called *How to Make Potions*. Nicole was reading a book called *How to Speak Gypsy Language.*

"Monique, I know how you say hello in Romani: *Dobraj tut*. It sounds like a magic word. *Dobraj tut, dobraj tut, dobraj tu-tu-tu*. I sound like a real gypsy!" said Nicole looking at the mirror with her mom's dress on.

Just then, Nicole had an idea. "What if we trick our moms by saying we want to go to the library to practice our multiplication tables tomorrow. Instead, we will actually go to the circus and see Madam Lavender."

"Do you think our moms will believe us?" Monique looked nervous.

"My mom loves it when I study math. I think she will believe us," Nicole said confidently.

"OK, it's a deal! I can't wait for tomorrow!"

Chapter 2: Going to the Circus

The next morning Nicole woke up really early. Her parents were not even up yet! Nicole woke up her parents by shaking them. When Nicole tried to wake up her dad, he snored like crazy. "Honkshoo, honkshoo, honshoo..."

"WAKE UP DADDY!"

"What!!! It's 5:00, Nicole!"

"Er....sorry Daddy. I didn't mean to wake you up. I am just so excited."

"Excited about what?" asked Mr. Ruby.

"Um...nothing really. I want to go study multiplication in the library with Monique. Pleeeeaaaase can I go?"

"Okay, you can go to the library if you go back to sleep and stop bugging me."

Four hours later, Nicole woke up again. Her parents were downstairs. Nicole immediately picked up the phone and called her friend.

"Good morning, Monique. Did your mom say yes?" Nicole asked quickly.

"She said yes! I'll meet you at the bus stop in 20 minutes!" Monique excitedly said.

Nicole got ready in a few seconds because she already had what she needed: a bag full of her gypsy books, a watch, some necklaces, earrings, a shawl and a dollar bill. Nicole grabbed her bag and rushed out the door.

"Bye mom and dad!" yelled Nicole, waving. "I'll be home at 5:00!"

Chapter 3: Mixing it Up

When they got to the circus Nicole and Monique saw Madame Lavender's tent from the entrance. It looked exactly the same as last year and was in the same spot. They ran straight to it and went inside. Everything was the same except for one thing: no gypsy. They looked around the dark, gloomy tent. There was a pot, some potions, and a small table with a crystal ball.

"This is amazing," Monique said, "even though there's no gypsy."

"Why don't we make some potions? I know how to make a few...at least I think I can," said Nicole somewhat uncertainly.

"We could," said Monique "If we are careful." She looked a little afraid.

"Don't worry. Let's have some fun!" said Nicole jumping up and with excitement.

Nicole and Monique started making potions. They mixed and mixed and the potions bubbled and bubbled. Finally they were done with a dozen potions. They were both dripping with sweat.

"That was a lot of hard work," said Nicole.

Suddenly, they heard a voice.

"Hello, my name is Jerry. What's your name?"

Nicole quickly said, "My name is Madam Lavender and this is my assistant, Rosemary."

"Wow, both of you have flower names," said Jerry. "How old are you? You look very young."

Nicole hastily explained, "We have been gypsies for a long time. We are actually old ladies. Last week we took a potion that made us look like little girls!"

But Jerry was not listening. Instead he asked, "May I have a potion that makes me have some hair? I'm going bald."

"How long do you want your hair to be?" Nicole grinned secretly, thinking about her experience last year.

"3 inches long," Jerry answered.

Nicole and Monique gave Jerry the potion they just made which was red and had ice in it. "$1 please!" said Nicole. "Here you go."

"Thank you!" Jerry said. "This is a great store! I'm going to tell all my friends!"

Nicole and Monique watched as Jerry walked further in the carnival shouting, "POTIONS FOR $1.00 EACH! MAGIC GYPSY KIDS! POTIONS FOR $1.00 EACH! MAGIC GYPSY KIDS! "

Nicole and Monique looked at each other and sighed. "Oh, no."

Chapter 4: The Big Mistake

The room was flooded within seconds. Customers were everywhere! They were babbling about what potion they would get. It looked like a mass of swarming ants. One by one, Nicole and Monique gave a potion to every customer. By noon time, they had already sold 3 dozen potions. There were no more potions left! Nicole and Monique were about to close the tent when they heard a noise outside.

"Help, help, help!"

Nicole and Monique immediately recognized that voice. It was the voice they had heard 4 hours ago: Jerry's.

"Help I have hair on my back! AAAAAAAAHHHHHHHH!"

Nicole and Monique ran out of the tent, surprised to see Jerry scratching his back like a monkey.

"Get this off of me!" he wailed.

"Calm down Jerry," Nicole (acting as Madam Lavender) soothed. "It's OK, just calm down."

Jerry shouted, "No! You're the

people who did it! You're horrible gypsies! I don't think you're gypsies anyway!"

Nicole and Monique gulped. That was their big secret.

"Yeah, you're not!" An angry mob of customers walked straight at Nicole and Monique. They were like a raging rhino!

Nicole and Monique could recognize all the customers, but there was something very strange about each one.

The lady who wanted straight teeth, got teeth straight down to her heart.

The man who wanted blue eyes got a blue mask.

The lady who wanted balloon lips got balloons on her lips.

The child who wanted wings got tiny butterfly wings.

The girl who wanted a big smile got a smile from ear to ear.

The man who wanted to speak Japanese could no longer speak English. "たすけて.." he screamed.

"What have we done?" Nicole whispered to Monique.

They were feeling like they would be doomed in a second. With all of these adults running at them, they just felt like running away. Just then, matters got even worse. In the distance, Nicole could see her parents walking into the circus. They did not look happy at all.

Nicole was very frightened and Monique was feeling miserable for her friend. She knew Nicole was about to get in big, big trouble.

"What was that gypsy word?" Nicole asked Monique.

"I think it was *tut dobraj….*"

That is when things got very weird.

Chapter 5: Madam Lavender

Suddenly, there was a loud poof and an enormous cloud of foggy grey smoke appeared right in front of them. Everyone stopped to look at the cloud of smoke. A shadowy figure appeared in the fog and took a few steps forward. The crowd gasped. It was a lady, an older lady, and she was wearing a shawl and a tremendous amount of jewelry. She smiled at Nicole.

"*Bingo!*" Nicole thought to herself. "I *know* who that is!"

"Madam Lavender?" Nicole said uncertainly.

Madam Lavender spoke. "Hello, Nicole. Did you have a good time being a gypsy? Didn't you notice a cat following you around this whole day?"

Nicole stammered "I...I...I...did see a cat. That was you?"

"Yes, dear that was me. When you said *'Dobraj tut'* that meant 'I want to be a gypsy'. When you said it yesterday, you changed me into a cat so you could become a gypsy. When your friend said *'tut dobraj'* she undid the spell. You have made some terrible mistakes today," Madam Lavender replied.

Just then, Madam Lavender started walking around the crowd. She took out some sparkling blue and pink powder from a pouch around her neck. She went from person to person, sprinkling the powder on the heads of all the people who had taken potions from Nicole and Monique.

"I can fly!" said the child who now had perfect blue and purple wings.

"My blue eyes look great!" said the man who wanted blue eyes but had gotten a blue mask.

"I can speak English again! にほんごもできる！" said the man who wanted speak Japanese but had lost the power to speak English.

Soon enough, everyone had gotten the wish they were supposed to be granted. They all thanked Madam Lavender and rushed off to show their families what had happened.

"Nicole, we need to talk," her parents said.

Chapter 6: Future Gypsy

"Nicole, I am very disappointed in you. You lied to us about going to the library to study your multiplication tables. You came to the circus instead. On top of that, you pretended to be a gypsy and made all those people look foolish. You should be ashamed of yourself," Mr. Ruby angrily said.

"I am very, very sorry. I didn't mean to cause this much trouble. I promise not to lie anymore," Nicole replied meaningfully.

"Me too," Monique said solemnly.

"Nicole, you're grounded for one month. And Monique, I will tell your parents about everything that has happened today. It will be up to them to decide what to do." Mr. Ruby looked at both of them.

Madam Lavender spoke next. "Nicole, you're going to be a famous gypsy someday, but you have to be careful. Don't play with gypsy things when you do not know what they are."

"OK, Madam Lavender. I understand. I just love gypsies and learning everything about them."

Madam Lavender looked at Nicole's parents. "Your child is special. I think she has natural ability. Would you let Nicole join my gypsy school next summer? The school lasts for three weeks. She would learn what the secret ingredient is and how to make lots of potions that will make people happy."

Nicole felt butterflies in her stomach. She hoped her Mom and Dad would say yes.

"It is OK with us, as long as she behaves well all next year." Mr. and Mrs. Ruby smiled.

"THANK YOU MOM AND DAD! I love you so much. Madam Lavender, I would love to go to gypsy school. Thank you for inviting me." Nicole beamed.

"You're welcome, Nicole. You will need to work hard. Take this book about the secret ingredient.

After you read this book, you can come to my gypsy school." Madam Lavender gave Nicole the book.

Nicole hugged Madam Lavender.

"Thank you so much for the book. You are the best. I promise I won't turn you into a cat again!" Nicole giggled.

"Time to go Nicole and Monique. It's getting late," Mrs. Ruby said.

"Goodbye, Madam Lavender. Thank you for being so kind," Monique and Nicole said. Finally they walked merrily out of the circus and into the twinkling, starry night.

To Be Continued…

About the Author

Jacqueline Fowler is seven years old. She is a 2nd grader in James Franklin Smith Elementary School. This is her second book. Her first book was called The Girl Who Wanted Long Hair. She loves to read books (especially first thing in the morning!), dance, and travel to different places. Someday she hopes to go to Italy. She lives in San Jose, California with her parents, sister and her imaginary mouse.

Proof

6224162R0